To Jim, Salty, Ollie and Lara. K.G.

For Mum and Dad, who I can always count on! J.F.

First published in 2015 by Hodder Children's Books

Text copyright © Kes Gray 2015
Illustration copyright © Jim Field 2015

Hodder Children's Books
338 Euston Road, London NW1 3BH

Hodder Children's Books Australia
Level 17/207 Kent Street, Sydney, NSW 2000

A catalogue record of this book is available from the British Library.

ISBN: 978 1 444 91096 4
10 9 8 7 6 5 4 3 2

Printed in Spain

Hodder Children's Books is a division of Hachette Children's Books.
An Hachette UK Company

www.hachette.co.uk

HOW MANY LEGS?

Kes Gray and **Jim Field**

How many legs would there be

if in this room there was only me?

How many legs would there be
If a **polar bear** came for tea?

How many legs would it make
If a **duck** arrived with a lemon cake?

How many legs would be on view
If a **hippo** was invited too?

How many legs would you see if a **dog** walked in with a **chimpanzee?**

How many legs would be found
If a **seagull** joined us on the ground?

What would all
the legs come to
if a **frog** hopped in
on a **kangaroo**?

POP!

How high would the leg count go
If a **squid** rode in
on a **buffalo**?

How many legs would there be

If a **flea** flew in on a **bumble bee?**

Would the leg
count go right up
if an **octopus** and
a **pig** turned up?

Why would the number stay the same if a **slug**, a **snail** and a **maggot** came?

How would the number multiply
If a **centipede** came wiggling by?

How many legs would you find
If a **COW** walked in with a **goat** behind?

Leg-wise, what would be the score

if we were joined by a **dinosaur**?

4 + 2 + 2 + 2 + 2 +

8 + 4 + 0 + 100

If you lose count don't feel bad,
A sum this big could send you mad.
No need to tie your brain in knots,
Let's just say the answer's...

The correct answer is...